A WHALE IN THE BATHTUB

by Kylie Westaway Illustrated by Tom Jellett

CLARION BOOKS | Houghton Mifflin Harcourt | Boston New York

For Mum and Dad, for always believing in me.
And for Flynn, who inspired the story, and for Bruno,
who lent me his name —K.W.

For Lucy and Ted —T.J.

CLARION BOOKS
215 Park Avenue South
New York, New York 10003

First published in Australia in 2014 by Allen & Unwin
First U.S. edition 2016

Clarion Books is an imprint of Houghton Mifflin Harcourt Publishing Company.

www.hmhco.com

The text was set in Legacy Sans ITC Std.

Library of Congress Cataloging-in-Publication Data is available.
ISBN 978-0-544-53535-0

Manufactured in China
SCP 10 9 8 7 6 5 4 3 2 1
4500582445

Tonight there was a **whale** in our bathtub.
He was using my bubble bath.

"You could have knocked!" he said.

I'd never seen a **whale**
in our bathtub before.
I wanted to ask how he got there.

"You're using my bubblegum
bubble bath," I said.

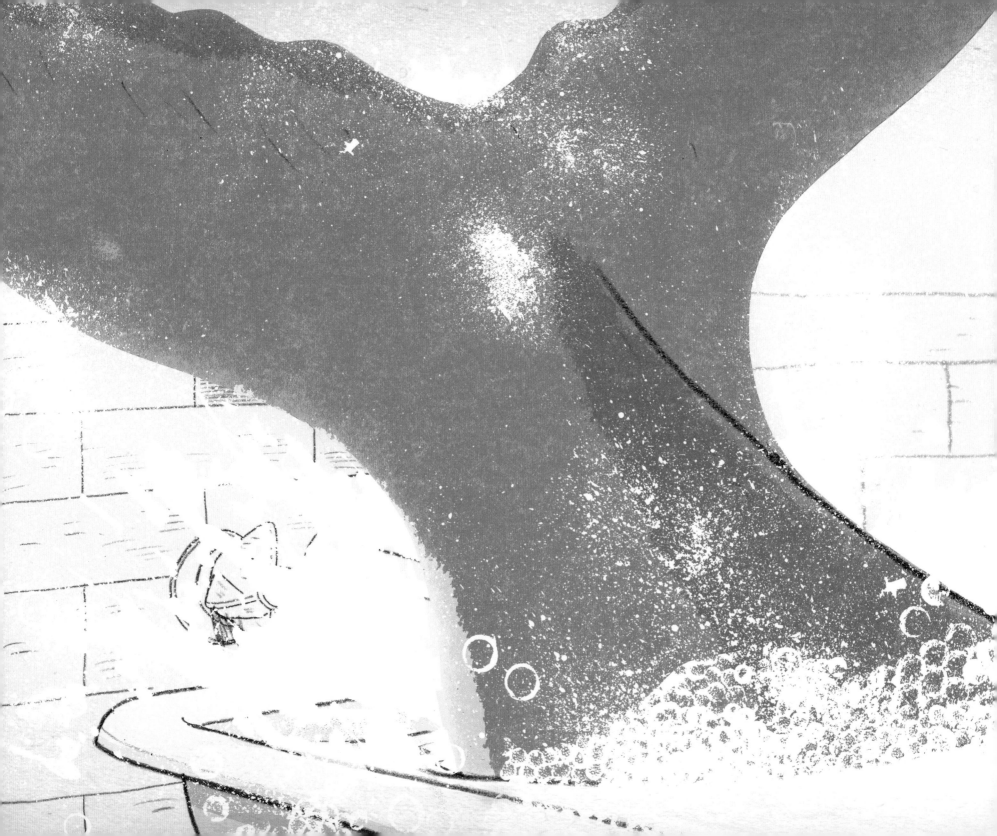

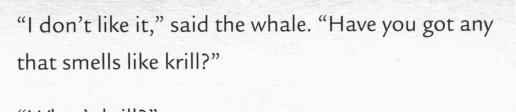

"I don't like it," said the whale. "Have you got any that smells like krill?"

"What's krill?"

"Krill's my favorite food. And can you shut the door? You're letting the heat out."

My sister, Ally, was watching TV.

"Mom told you to get in the bathtub, Bruno."

"I can't," I told her. "There's a **whale** in our bathtub."

"Mom," shouted Ally, "Bruno's pretending again!
And he's not taking a bath!"

"I'm not pretending."

"Last week you said there was a **BEAR** under your bed. On Dad's birthday, there was a **WALRUS** in the backyard. You're always making things up."

"Ally, stop telling tales," Mom said.
"Bruno, get in the bathtub!"

I **STOMPED** upstairs and **BANGED** on the bathroom door.

The **whale** was scrubbing under his flippers with Dad's back scrubber.

I frowned at the whale.

"I have to take my bath."

"I haven't done my tail yet. Come back later." He SQUIRTED in more bubble bath.

My brother loves science, and his room is always
full of rockets and robots and switches and tubes.

"Pete, there's a **whale** in our bathtub!"

"A **whale** can't fit in a bathtub," said Pete. "Even a baby whale would be too big. And there'd be no room for the water. It's just impossible."

I sighed. Then I asked, "Hey, Pete, what does krill smell like?"

But Pete was busy again.

I wandered back to the bathroom.

"I'm still washing my back," said the whale.

"Can't you wash in the ocean?" I asked.

"No hot water in the ocean," said the whale.

"And no bubble bath, or soap, or washcloths."

"But you're taking forever!"

"It'd be quicker if you had a bigger bathtub.
I feel like I'm washing in a bucket!"

He flicked bubbles at me.

"Come back later."

Dad was home when I went back downstairs.

He put down his suitcase and threw me up in the air.

"Dad, there's a whale in our bathtub!"

"A **whale**? Wow!" Dad laughed.
"How did it get there? Was there a flood
today and the whale got stranded? Or
did it just swim up through the drain?"

"I don't know, but I can't take my bath."

"Go on up, Bruno," said Dad. "It's bath time.
I'll be coming to check in five minutes."

"But Dad . . ."

"Now, Bruno!"

"Okay," I said to the whale, "you've had
a really long bath, and it's my turn now."

"No," said the whale, rinsing his barnacles.
"I'll be at least another hour. Maybe four."

"But I'll get in trouble! I have to take my bath!"

The whale looked at me and smiled. "I have an **IDEA**."

And the whale took a **LONG**,

DEEP breath.

Mom came up to tuck me in.

"You smell a bit fishy!" she said as she gave me a hug.

"It's probably krill," I said.

"Did you take your bath?"

"No," I said. "Tonight I had a shower."

Mom smiled. "Bruno, we don't have a shower."

"I know," I said. "But . . ."

". . . we do have a **whale** in our bathtub!"

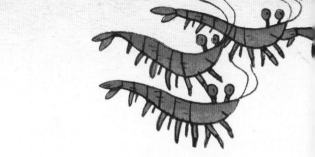